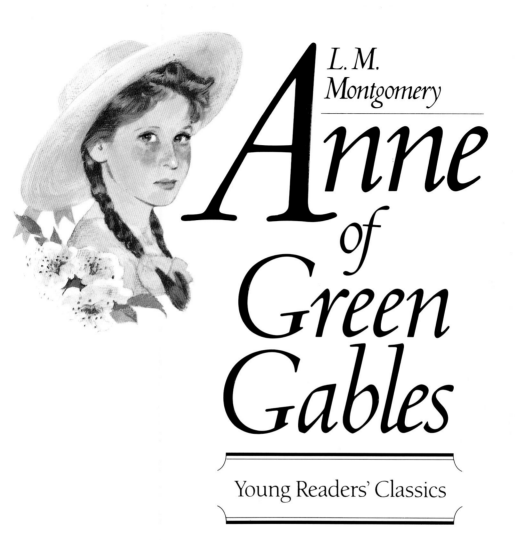

L. M. Montgomery

Anne of Green Gables

Young Readers' Classics

Abridgement by
Barbara Greenwood

Illustrations by Muriel Wood

KEY PORTER·BOOKS

Canadian Cataloguing in Publication Data

Montgomery, L.M. (Lucy Maud), 1874-1942
Anne of Green Gables.

ISBN 1-55013-354-3 (Hardcover)
ISBN 1-55013-431-0 (Paperback)

I. Greenwood, Barbara, 1940- . II. Wood,
Muriel. III. Title.

PS8526.045A75 1991   jC813'.52   C91-093530-0
PZ7.M66Ann 1991

Key Porter Books Limited
70 The Esplanade
Toronto, Ontario
Canada M5E 1R2

Typesetting: MacTrix DTP
Printed and bound in Hong Kong

1

Anne sat tensely on the pile of shingles, staring up and down the empty platform. The train had left the station long since and still no one had come for her. She grasped the handle of her shabby, old-fashioned carpet bag, and searched, with large grey-green eyes, for any sign of life. Then, just as the ticketmaster was locking the front door of the station, a horse and buggy rattled up.

At last, she sighed, and her heart calmed a little. A man with a long, full beard clambered down. He looks kindly, she thought, and her eyes followed him as he sidled past her without even a glance and went up to the stationmaster. She strained to catch words from the low murmuring. Suddenly she heard, "Well, she's the only one got off the train." They both looked her way and the bearded man shrugged.

He must be for me, Anne thought desperately and jumped to her feet. "I suppose you are Mr. Matthew Cuthbert of Green Gables." She held out her hand as she had been taught. "I'm very glad to see you. I was afraid you weren't coming for me and I was imagining what I'd do. I thought I'd climb up that big wild cherry tree at the bend. I wouldn't be a bit afraid to sleep there."

He blinked, still holding her hand, then said shyly, "I'm sorry I was late. Come along. The horse is over there. Give me your bag."

"Oh, I can carry it. It isn't a bit heavy." She grasped the shabby bag and followed him. "I'm very glad you've come. It seems so wonderful that I'm going to live with you and belong to you. I've never belonged to anyone – not really."

The man glanced at her and then away again as he swung her bag into the buggy. Anne felt nervous all of a sudden and rattled on, "The asylum was the worst. I don't suppose you've ever been an orphan in an asylum. I was only there four months, but it was worse than anything you can imagine." He said nothing, just waited until she had settled herself on

the seat and then clucked to the horse. I'd better not talk, Anne decided, folding her hands in her lap. The buggy lurched and they were off.

As they bumped along in silence, Anne gazed around her. They had left the village and were driving down a steep hill, the road part of which had been cut so deeply into the soft soil that the banks, fringed with blooming wild cherry trees and slim white birches, made an archway several feet above their heads.

"Oh, Mr. Cuthbert! Oh, Mr. Cuthbert!" Anne exclaimed, her thin hands clasped before her, her face lifted rapturously to the white splendour above. "Did you ever see anything so wonderful? It's the first thing I ever saw that couldn't be improved by imagination. I always heard Prince Edward Island was the prettiest place in the world. I just love it already. I'm so glad I'm going to live here."

Matthew cleared his throat. "Well now . . ." He gave her such a sad look that Anne said quickly, "Am I talking too much? People are always telling me I do. I can stop when I make up my mind to it, although it's difficult. Would you like me to stop?"

"Oh, you can talk as much as you like. I don't mind."

"I'm so glad. I know you and I are going to get along together fine. It's such a relief to talk when one wants and not be told children should be seen and not heard. People laugh at me because I use big words but if you have big ideas, you have to use big words, don't you?"

"Well now, that does seem reasonable."

"Do you know," Anne said, her thoughts darting off in another direction, "my arm must be all black and blue. I was so afraid this was all a dream I had to keep pinching myself to see if it was real. But it is real. And we're nearly home."

"Well now . . ." Matthew sounded so uncomfortable that Anne turned to stare at him.

"Yes, Mr. Cuthbert?"

He looked away. "Marilla – that's my sister – she'll . . . she'll tell you all about things." He clucked to the horse and the buggy bounded forward.

When they had driven up a further hill and around a corner, Matthew said, "We're pretty near home now. That's Green Gables over – "

"Oh, don't tell me," Anne interrupted breath-

lessly. She looked down the crest of the hill. To the west a dark church spire rose up against a marigold sky. Down the slope of the hill were scattered snug farmsteads. From one to another Anne's eyes darted, eager and wistful. At last they lingered on one far back from the road, where white blossoming trees stood out against the twilight of the surrounding woods.

"That's it, isn't it?" she said pointing.

Matthew slapped the reins on the sorrel's back delightedly. "Well now, you guessed it."

With a sigh of rapture, Anne relapsed into silence. They drove over the Hollow, up the hill, and into the long lane to Green Gables. The yard was quite dark as they turned into it and the poplar leaves were rustling silkily all around.

"Listen to the trees talking in their sleep," Anne whispered as Matthew lifted her to the ground. "What nice dreams they must have!"

Then, holding tightly to the carpetbag, she followed him into the house.

A tall thin woman with dark hair twisted up into a hard little knot stood in the middle of the parlour.

Anne's heart pounded. She clutched her bag to

her chest. The woman came forward briskly, then stopped in amazement, staring at Anne.

"Matthew Cuthbert, who is this?" she exclaimed. "Where is the boy?"

"There wasn't any boy," Matthew said wretchedly. "There was only *her*."

"There must have been a boy. We sent word by Mrs. Spencer to bring a boy."

During this dialogue Anne had remained silent, her eyes roving from one to the other. Suddenly she grasped the meaning of what was being said. "You don't want me?" she cried. "You don't want me because I'm not a boy! I might have known nobody really wanted me. Oh, what shall I do?" Covering her face with her hands she burst into noisy sobs.

Brother and sister looked at each other in dismay. Finally Marilla said lamely, "Now there's no need to cry so about it."

"Oh, but there is." Anne wiped her eyes with the backs of her hands. "You would cry too if you had come to a place you thought was going to be home and they didn't want you because you weren't a boy. This is the most tragical thing that has ever happened to me."

A tiny smile tugged at Marilla's mouth. "Well, don't cry any more. We're not going to turn you out-of-doors tonight. You'll have to stay here until we've investigated this affair. What's your name?"

"Anne Shirley." She hesitated for a moment, then said quickly, "And would you please call me Anne spelled with an 'e'?"

"What difference does it make how it's spelled?"

"When I hear my name, I see it printed out in my mind. And A-n-n-e looks so much nicer."

"Very well then, Anne with an 'e'," Marilla snapped in exasperation, "can you tell me how this mistake came to be made? Were there no boys at the orphanage?"

"Oh, yes, plenty. But when Mrs. Spencer came with your message she *distinctly* said a girl about eleven years old. And the matron said she thought I would do. I was so delighted. I couldn't sleep last night for joy." She turned suddenly to Matthew. "Why didn't you tell me at the station? Why didn't you leave me there? It's so much harder now that I've seen Green Gables."

Hesitantly Matthew put a hand out to Anne, then backed away. "I'll put the mare in, Marilla," he

mumbled. "Have tea ready when I get back."

"Did Mrs. Spencer bring anybody besides you?" Marilla continued when Matthew had gone out.

"She brought Lily Jones for herself. Lily is five and has beautiful nut brown hair. Would you keep me if I had nut brown hair instead of this horrible red?" Anne shook her long braids at Marilla.

"A girl is no use to us at all," Marilla said severely. "We need a boy to help Matthew with the farm work. Now take your hat off and put it with your bag on the hall table. We'll talk about this after supper."

Anne felt so unhappy that she could only nibble at the bread and butter and crab apple jam.

"I guess she's tired," said Matthew. "Best put her to bed." So Anne followed Marilla up the stairs to a tiny room in the east gable under the roof. Marilla set the candle on the edge of a small table and turned the bedclothes down. "Undress as quick as you can," she said. "I'll have to wait for the candle. I daren't trust you to put it out yourself. You'd have the place on fire. Good night," she said as Anne burrowed down into the pillow and pulled the blankets over her head.

How can it be a good night? It is the very worst night I've ever had, Anne thought to herself. Lying rigidly in bed she listened to the sounds of the house, little stirrings and creakings, a door closing and then Marilla's voice carrying clearly up the stairs, "This is a pretty kettle of fish. This is what comes of sending word instead of going ourselves."

A deeper voice murmured something and was cut off by Marilla's. "Keep her? You know very well we need a boy to help with the farm. What good would *she* be to us?" And then there was silence throughout the house.

In the east gable bedroom, Anne buried her face in the pillow and cried herself to sleep.

2

The next afternoon Anne and Marilla set out in the horse and buggy for White Sands, to talk to Mrs. Spencer.

"I've made up my mind to enjoy this drive," Anne announced as they turned out of the gate. "I'm not going to think even once about the orphanage. Oh, look! There's an early wild rose. Don't you think it would be nice if roses could talk? I'm sure they could tell us such lovely things. And don't you think pink is a lovely colour? Redheaded people can't wear pink. Not even in their imagination. Did you ever know of anybody whose hair was red when she was young, but got to be another colour when she grew up?"

"No, I never did. And I don't think it's likely to

happen to you, either."

"Another hope gone." Anne sighed. "My life is a perfect graveyard of buried hopes. I read that sentence in a book once. I say it over to comfort myself whenever I'm disappointed."

"I don't see where the comforting comes in, myself."

"Because it sounds so nice. And it makes me see pictures in my mind. White Sands does that, too. And Avonlea. Avonlea sounds just like music. How far is it to White Sands?"

"Five miles – and since you're bent on talking you might as well tell me what you know about yourself."

"I'd much rather tell you what I imagine about myself."

"Just you stick to bald facts. Begin at the beginning. Where were you born, and how old are you?"

"I was eleven last March," Anne began obediently. "I was born in Bolingbroke, Nova Scotia. My mother and father were both teachers in the high school. Mrs. Thomas who brought me up said they were as poor as church mice and that I was the ugliest baby she'd ever seen, but that my mother thought I

was perfectly beautiful. I guess a mother should know that better than a lady who came in to clean. But then they both died of fever and nobody wanted me, so Mrs. Thomas took me even though she was poor and had a drunken husband. She kept me until I was eight and I helped with all four of her children, but then her husband fell under a train and she had to go and live with her mother. There was no room for me so Mrs. Hammond from up the river said she'd take me since I was good with children. Mrs. Hammond had twins *three* times. I used to get dreadfully tired carrying them all about. But then they moved to the States and didn't want me, so I was sent to the orphanage. I *am* good with children. I wish you had some so I could show you," Anne finished with a sigh.

"Did you never go to school?"

"Not very much. Mostly it was too far to walk. But of course I did last year when I was at the orphanage. I can read pretty well and I know ever so many pieces of poetry off by heart."

Marilla looked at Anne out of the corner of her eye. "Those women, Mrs. Thomas and Mrs. Hammond, were they good to you?"

"O-o-o-h," Anne faltered. Her sensitive face

flushed scarlet with embarrassment. "They *meant* to be. I know they meant to be. But they had a good deal to worry them, you know."

Marilla asked no more questions. She just tightened her lips and looked severe. They drove in silence until Marilla turned the horse in at a big yellow house beside the sea.

Mrs. Spencer came to the door with surprise and welcome mingled on her face. "Why, Marilla Cuthbert, Anne, you're the last folks I was looking for today."

"We can't stay, Mrs. Spencer, but the fact is there's been a mistake somewhere and I've come over to see where it is. We sent word, Matthew and I, for you to bring us a boy from the orphanage. A boy ten or eleven years old to help Matthew on the farm."

"Why, Robert sent word by his daughter Nancy that you wanted a girl. Isn't that so, Flora Jane?" She turned to her daughter who had come out onto the steps.

"She certainly did, Miss Cuthbert."

"I'm dreadful sorry," Mrs. Spencer continued, "but it wasn't my fault. I did the best I could."

"It was our own fault," Marilla said resignedly.

"We should have come down ourselves with such an important message. But what am I to do now? Can I send the child back to the orphanage?"

"I suppose so." Mrs. Spencer thought for a moment. "But maybe it won't be necessary. Mrs. Peter Blewett was saying just yesterday she wished she'd sent for a girl to help her. She has a large family. Anne will be the very girl for her."

"That woman!" Marilla snorted. "I wouldn't give a *dog* I liked to that woman." She looked at Anne who was listening as hard as she could to this strange conversation. Then she looked back at Mrs. Spencer. "Well, now," she said thoughtfully, "Matthew and I haven't absolutely decided that we wouldn't keep her. I feel I shouldn't decide anything without consulting him. We'll just go home and think it over."

Anne had been trying so hard not to hope, as Marilla worked her way slowly through this speech, that she thought she would burst. "Oh, Miss Cuthbert, did you really say that perhaps you would let me stay at Green Gables?" she whispered breathlessly. "Did you really? Or did I just imagine it?"

"I think you had better learn to control that imagination of yours, Anne," Marilla said crossly. "You heard me say just that and no more. It isn't decided yet."

By the next afternoon Anne couldn't wait another moment. As soon as Matthew went out after dinner she turned to Marilla. "Oh, please, Miss Cuthbert, won't you tell me if you're going to send me away? I've tried to be patient, but I just can't bear waiting any longer."

"I suppose I might as well tell you. Matthew and I have decided that if you're a good girl and show yourself grateful – well, then we'll keep you. Why ever are you crying, child?"

"I don't know," Anne wailed. "I'm as glad as can be, so why *am* I crying?"

"Sit down and calm yourself, child."

"What am I to call you?" Anne asked when the tears had finally stopped. "Can I call you Aunt Marilla? I'd love to call you that."

"You'll call me plain Marilla like everyone else in Avonlea."

"Couldn't we imagine you're my aunt?"

"No, we couldn't. I don't believe in calling people names that don't belong to them."

"But I've never had an aunt."

"The first thing you'd better learn, Anne, is that when I tell you something, I want you to obey me. Now come and help me finish these dinner dishes."

Anne had been two weeks at Green Gables when Marilla called her up to her bedroom one morning.

"Well, how do you like them?" Spread out on the bed were three new dresses. One was a sandy brown gingham, one was a black and white sateen and the third was a bright blue print. Each had a plain skirt gathered into a plain top with straight, narrow sleeves.

"I'll imagine I like them," Anne said soberly, after a long look.

"I don't want you to imagine it," Marilla said huffily. "What's the matter with them? Aren't they clean and neat and new?"

"Yes."

"Then why don't you like them?"

"They're not . . . they're not pretty," Anne said reluctantly.

"Pretty!" Marilla sniffed. "They're good, sensible,

serviceable dresses without frills or furbelows. That sateen will do you for church and the others are just what you need for starting school. I thought you'd be grateful after those skimpy things you brought from the orphanage."

"Oh, I am grateful. But I'd just be ever so much *more* grateful if one of them had been white with puffed sleeves."

"I haven't any material to waste on puffed sleeves. Besides, they look ridiculous. Now hang the dresses up ready for school. Oh, and the Barry girl's back home so you'll have somebody to walk with."

"A girl my own age? Oh, Marilla, what's her name? Do you think she'll be my best friend?"

"That will depend on Mrs. Barry. She's very particular who Diana plays with."

"Diana? Diana Barry? What a perfectly beautiful name. I just know we are going to be best friends and kindred spirits."

3

Anne was trembling as she walked with Marilla the next day through the orchard, by the short cut across the bridge and up the hill to the Barrys' kitchen door.

"Now remember, Anne, you must be polite and well-behaved. None of your startling speeches."

"Oh, Marilla, I'm frightened, actually frightened. What if Diana doesn't like me? It would be the most tragical disappointment of my life."

"I guess Diana will like you well enough. It's her mother you've got to reckon with. If *she* doesn't like you, it won't matter how much Diana does."

Mrs. Barry came to the back door in answer to Marilla's knock. "Come in, Marilla. And this is the little girl you've adopted, I guess. How are you, Anne?"

"I'm well in body, though considerably rumpled in spirit, thank you, ma'am." Anne caught Marilla looking at her, and closed her mouth on her next words.

Diana was sitting on the sofa reading a book which she dropped as the visitors entered.

"Diana, you might take Anne into the garden to show her your flowers," Mrs. Barry said as Anne gazed, mesmerized, at Diana's long, shiny, black hair and rosy cheeks. Anne followed Diana into the garden, for once having nothing to say. The girls wandered through beds filled with tiger lilies and crimson peonies, taking shy little glances at each other.

"Oh, Diana," Anne burst out at last, clasping her hands and speaking almost in a whisper, "do you think you can like me a little – enough to be my bosom friend?"

Diana laughed. "Why, I guess so. I'm awfully glad you've come to live at Green Gables. There isn't any other girl who lives near enough to play with."

"Will you swear to be my friend for ever and ever?"

"It's dreadfully wicked to swear."

"Oh, no, not *my* kind of swearing. It just means

vowing and promising solemnly."

"Well, I don't mind that," agreed Diana, relieved. "How do you do it?"

"We must join our hands – so. It should be over running water. We'll just have to imagine that. I'll repeat the oath first. I solemnly swear to be faithful to my bosom friend, Diana Barry, as long as the sun and moon shall endure. Now you say it and put my name in it."

Diana repeated the oath with a laugh. Then she said, "You're a strange girl, Anne, but I believe I'm going to like you."

By the time school started Anne and Diana were truly bosom friends. They did everything together, even reading out of the same book, page about. On the way to school each day they compared the dinners they carried in baskets over their arms, put their bottles of milk side by side in the brook to keep cool and sweet until dinner hour, then sat in the same double desk to do their work. Anne thought she was the happiest girl in Avonlea.

One day as they walked down the school path together Diana said, "I guess Gilbert Blythe will be in school today. He's been visiting his cousins over in

New Brunswick and he only came home Saturday night. He's awfully handsome. He teases the girls something terrible and he's always head of the class. You won't find it so easy to be first after this, Anne."

"I'm glad," Anne said quickly. "I couldn't feel proud of keeping ahead of little boys and girls of nine and ten. I came first yesterday spelling 'ebullition.' That Josie Pye peeped in her speller and even then she couldn't spell it right."

"Those Pye girls are all cheats. Look, there's Gilbert. Don't you think he's handsome?"

A tall boy, with brown hair, roguish hazel eyes and a mouth twisted into a teasing smile, was coming around the side of the school. As he saw the girls he winked, then turned in at the door.

"He's handsome enough," Anne admitted. "But I think he's very bold. It isn't good manners to wink at a strange girl."

Anne spent the whole morning ignoring Gilbert Blythe who seemed to be trying to catch her eye for another bold wink. In the afternoon she had actually forgotten his existence and was staring out the window in the middle of a beautiful daydream when she felt someone lift one long braid.

"Carrots! Carrots!" came a piercing whisper and with each word came a tug on the braid.

Anne sprang to her feet, her eyes sparkling with angry tears. "You mean, hateful boy. How dare you?" And then – thwack – she brought her writing slate down on Gilbert's head. The slate cracked clear across.

Diana gasped. Everyone turned to stare in horrified delight, as the teacher, Mr. Phillips, stalked down the aisle.

"Anne Shirley, what does this mean?"

Anne tightened her lips and said nothing. She would never, never repeat to anyone what *that boy* had called her.

Gilbert spoke up. "It was my fault, Mr. Phillips. I teased her."

The teacher paid no attention to Gilbert. "I am sorry," he said stiffly, "to see a pupil of mine display such a temper. Go and stand on the platform in front of the blackboard, Anne, for the rest of the afternoon."

Her face white and set, Anne obeyed. What could be worse than to be made a spectacle in front of the whole class! Mr. Phillips wrote on the blackboard

above her head, "Ann Shirley must learn to control her temper." Then, just to make sure even the youngest understood, he read it aloud to the class.

Anne stood rigid. She didn't cry or hang her head. Her cheeks red with anger, she stared resentfully both at Diana's sympathetic gaze and Josie Pye's malicious smile. But she deliberately looked away from Gilbert Blythe, vowing silently, I'll never, never speak to him again.

When school was dismissed Anne marched out with her head held high. Gilbert was waiting for her on the porch.

"I'm awfully sorry I made fun of your hair, Anne," he whispered. "Honest I am. Please don't be mad for keeps."

Anne swept past without a sign of seeing or hearing.

"How could you, Anne? Just ignore him like that?" panted Diana when she finally caught up with her. "And anyway, Gilbert makes fun of all the girls. He's called me 'crow' a dozen times. And I've never heard him apologize before."

"There's a great deal of difference between being called crow and being called carrots," said Anne with dignity. "Gilbert Blythe has hurt my feelings *excruciatingly*. I shall never forgive him. And Mr. Phillips spelled my name without an 'e'. I have made up my mind, Diana. I am not coming back to school any more."

When Marilla heard the whole story she declared "Insulted fiddlesticks! You'll go to school tomorrow as usual."

"From what I've heard," Matthew said, "that Mr.

Phillips isn't any good at all as a teacher." Then he went back to fumbling with his pipe as Marilla glared at him.

Anne just shook her head gently. "I'm not going back, Marilla. I'll learn my lessons at home and I'll be as good as I can and hold my tongue all the time if it's possible. But I will *not* go back to school."

And there the matter stayed. Marilla stopped arguing and Anne stayed home. She learned her lessons, did her chores and played with Diana in the chilly autumn twilight; but when she met Gilbert Blythe on the road or at Sunday School she turned her face away and passed him by with icy contempt. No matter what he tried to say or what Diana said, Anne had made up her mind to hate Gilbert to the end of life.

4

One Saturday morning in October Marilla announced that she was going to a meeting of the Ladies' Aid Society at Carmody, five miles away. "I likely won't be home before dark. You'll have to get Matthew his supper and if you like you can ask Diana to come over and have tea with you."

"Oh, Marilla," Anne clasped her hands. "How perfectly lovely! You *are* able to imagine things after all or you'd never have understood how I longed for that very thing. Oh, Marilla, can I use the rosebud spray tea set?"

"No, indeed! Whatever next? You know I never use that except for the minister or the Ladies' Aid Society. You use the old brown tea set. But you can open a little yellow crock of cherry preserves and cut fruitcake and set out some of the cookies."

"I can just imagine myself sitting down at the head of the table and pouring tea," said Anne shutting her eyes ecstatically. "And asking Diana if she takes sugar and pressing her to take another piece of fruitcake. Oh, Marilla, it's a wonderful sensation just to think of it. Can I take her into the parlour to sit?"

"No, the sitting room will do for you and your company. But you and Diana can have the raspberry cordial left over from the church social the other night, and a cookie to eat with it along in the afternoon, for I dare say Matthew'll be late coming into tea since he's hauling potatoes to the vessel."

Anne flew down the hollow and up the spruce path to ask Diana to tea. As a result, just after Marilla had driven off to Carmody, Diana came over, dressed in her second best dress and looking exactly as it is proper to look when asked out to tea. She knocked primly on the front door and when Anne, dressed in *her* second best dress, just as primly opened the door, the two girls shook hands as gravely as if they had never met before.

They spent most of the afternoon in the orchard, sitting in a grassy corner where the frost had spared the green, and the mellow autumn sunshine lingered warmly. Diana had much to tell Anne about what went on at school. She had to sit with Gertie Pye and Gertie squeaked her pencil all the time which just made her – Diana's – blood run cold. Ruby Gillis had charmed all her warts away with a magic pebble that old Mary Jo from the Creek had given her. Sam Boulter had 'sassed' Mr. Phillips in class and Mr. Phillips had whipped him and Gilbert Blythe –

But Anne didn't want to hear about Gilbert Blythe. She jumped up hurriedly and suggested they go in and have some raspberry cordial.

Anne looked on the second shelf of the sitting room pantry as Marilla had told her. No bottle of raspberry cordial was to be seen. She searched until she found it away back on the top shelf. Then she put it on a tray and set it on the table with a tumbler.

"Now, please help yourself, Diana," she said politely. "I don't believe I'll have any just now. I don't feel as if I want any after all those apples."

Diana poured herself out a tumblerful, looked at its bright red hue admiringly, then sipped it daintily.

"That's awfully nice, Anne. I didn't know raspberry cordial was so nice."

"I'm glad you like it. Take as much as you want. I'm going to run out and stir the fire up. There are so many responsibilities on a person's mind when they're keeping house, aren't there?"

When Anne came back from the kitchen Diana was drinking her second glassful of cordial. "Have another," she invited and Diana filled her glass again.

"The nicest I ever drank," said Diana. "Ever so much nicer than Mrs. Lynde's although she brags about hers so much."

"Much nicer than Mrs. Lynde's," Anne agreed loyally. "Marilla is a famous cook. She is trying to teach me to cook but I assure you, Diana, it is uphill work. There's so little scope for imagination in cookery. You just have to go by the rules. The last time I made a cake I forgot to put the flour in. I was imagining I was a frost fairy going through the woods turning the trees red and yellow, whichever they wanted to be, so I forgot the flour and the cake was a dismal failure. Flour is so essential to cakes. Marilla was very cross and I don't wonder. Why, Diana, what is the matter?"

Diana had stood up very unsteadily. Then she sat down again putting her hands to her head.

"I'm – I'm awful sick," she said a little thickly. "I – I – must go right home."

"Oh, you mustn't dream of going home without your tea," Anne cried in distress. "I'll go and put it on this very minute."

"I must go home," Diana repeated stupidly but determinedly. "I'm awful dizzy."

Anne, with tears of disappointment in her eyes, got Diana's hat and went with her as far as the Barry yard fence. Then she wept all the way back to Green Gables, where she put the remainder of the raspberry cordial back into the pantry and got tea ready for Matthew.

The next day was Sunday and as the rain poured down in torrents, Anne did not stir from Green Gables. Monday afternoon Marilla sent her down to the Barrys' on an errand. In a very short space of time Anne came flying back up the lane in tears. Into the kitchen she dashed and flung herself down on the sofa. "Whatever has gone wrong now, Anne," asked Marilla in dismay.

No answer from Anne except more tears and stormier sobs.

"Anne Shirley, when I ask you a question I want to be answered. Sit up this very minute."

Anne sat up. "Mrs. Barry was in an awful state. She says I set Diana *drunk* Saturday and sent her home in a disgraceful condition. She says I must be a thoroughly bad, wicked girl and she's never going to let Diana play with me again. Oh, Marilla, I'm just overcome with woe."

Marilla stared in blank amazement. "Set Diana drunk! Anne, are you or Mrs. Barry crazy? What did you give her?"

"Not a thing but raspberry cordial," sobbed Anne. "I never thought raspberry cordial would set people drunk."

"Drunk fiddlesticks!" said Marilla, marching to the sitting room pantry. When she returned with the bottle, her lips twitched into a smile in spite of herself. "Anne, you certainly do have a genius for getting into trouble. You went and gave Diana currant wine. Don't you know the difference?"

"I never tasted it. I thought it was the cordial. I meant to be so – so hospitable. And now Mrs. Barry believes I did it on purpose."

"Don't be foolish, Anne. You just go up this evening and tell her how it was."

When Anne presented herself, white-lipped and eager-eyed at Mrs. Barry's door she was met with a cold face.

"What do you want?" Mrs. Barry asked stiffly.

Anne clasped her hands. "Oh, Mrs. Barry, please forgive me. I did not mean to – to – intoxicate Diana. How could I? Just imagine if you were a poor little

orphan girl that kind people had adopted and you had just one bosom friend in all the world. Do you think you would intoxicate her on purpose? I thought it was only raspberry cordial. Oh, please don't say that you won't let Diana play with me any more. If you do you will cover my life with a cloud of woe."

As Anne talked Mrs. Barry's face grew stonier and stonier. "You needn't think you can get 'round me with your big words and flowery speeches, Anne Shirley. I don't think you are a fit girl for Diana to associate with. You'd better go home and be-have yourself."

Anne went back to Green Gables calm with despair. "My last hope is gone," she told Marilla. "Mrs. Barry treated me very insultingly. There's nothing left to do except pray and I don't know that God Himself can do very much with such an obstinate person as Mrs. Barry."

"Anne, you shouldn't say such things," Marilla said in a reproving tone but when Matthew said, from around the stem of his pipe, "Most unreasonable wo-man *I* ever saw," she made no effort to contradict him.

5

The following Monday Anne surprised Marilla by coming down from her room with her schoolbooks in her arms and her lips primmed up into a determined line.

"I'm going back to school," she announced. "That is all there is left in life for me, now that my friend has been ruthlessly torn from me. In school I can look at her and muse over days departed."

"You'd better muse over your lessons and sums," said Marilla tartly, although she looked pleased. "I hope we'll hear no more of breaking slates over people's heads and such carryings-on. Behave yourself and do just what your teacher tells you."

"I'll try to be a model pupil," agreed Anne dolefully. "There won't be much fun in it, I expect. Mr. Phillips said Minnie Andrews was a model student and there isn't a spark of imagination or life in her. But I feel so depressed that perhaps it will come easy to me. I'm going round by the road. I couldn't bear to go by the Birch Path all alone. I should weep bitter tears if I did."

Anne was welcomed back to school with open arms. Her imagination had been missed in games, her voice in the singing and her dramatic ability in the reading aloud of books at dinner hour. The only one who didn't seem to notice that Anne was back was Diana.

"She might just have smiled at me once," Anne mourned to Marilla that night. But the next morning a note, twisted and folded around a small parcel, was passed across to Anne.

> *Dear Anne,*
> Mother says I'm not to play or talk with you even in school. It isn't my fault and don't be cross at me, because I love you as much as ever. I miss you awfully to tell my secrets to. I made you one of the new bookmarks out of red tissue paper. They are awfully fashionable and only three girls in school know how to make them. When you look at it remember
> *Your true friend,*
> *Diana Barry*

Anne read the note, kissed the bookmark and sent a prompt reply back to the other side of the schoolroom.

My own darling Diana,
Of course I'm not cross at you because you have to obey your mother. Our spirits can commune. I shall keep your lovely present forever.

Yours until death us do part,
Anne Shirley

P.S. I shall sleep with your letter under my pillow tonight.

From that moment Anne flung herself into her studies heart and soul, determined that nothing, not even Mr. Phillips' bad teaching, would keep her back. She was especially determined not to be outdone by Gilbert Blythe. Soon everyone in class knew of their rivalry.

One day Gilbert headed the spelling class, the next Anne, with a toss of her long red braids, spelled him down. One morning Gilbert would have all his sums correct and his name written on the blackboard honour roll; the next morning Anne, having wrestled wildly with decimals the entire evening before, would be first. One awful day, to Anne's mortification, they were ties and their names were written up together. When the examinations were held at the end of each month the suspense was terrible. The first month, Gilbert came out three marks ahead – the second, Anne beat him by five. By the end of the term both were promoted into the fifth class and allowed to begin "the branches" – by which was meant Latin, French, algebra and geometry.

"Matthew, did you ever study geometry when you went to school?" Anne asked one January evening when Marilla had gone off to a meeting. They were sitting in the kitchen, Matthew on the sofa nodding over the *Farmers' Advocate* and Anne puzzling over her lessons. A bright fire glowed in the old-fashioned Waterloo stove and blue-white frost crystals shone on the window panes.

"Well now, no, I didn't," said Matthew, coming out of his doze with a start.

"I wish you had," Anne sighed, "because then you'd be able to sympathize with me. It's casting a cloud over my whole life. I'm such a dunce at it."

"Well now, I dunno," said Matthew soothingly. "I guess you're all right at anything. Mr. Phillips told me

last week in Blair's store in Carmody that you was the smartest scholar in school and making rapid progress. 'Rapid progress' was his very words."

"I'm sure I'd get on better with geometry if only he wouldn't change the letters," complained Anne. "I learn the proposition off by heart and then he draws it on the blackboard and puts different letters from what are in the book and I get all mixed up. I don't think a teacher should take such mean advantage, do you? Maybe I'll just run down to the cellar and get some russets. Would you like one?"

"Well now, I dunno but what I would," Matthew agreed.

Just as Anne grasped the knob of the cellar door, she heard the sound of flying footsteps on the icy board walk outside. The next moment the kitchen door was flung open and in rushed Diana Barry, white-faced and breathless, with a shawl wrapped hastily around her head.

"Whatever is the matter, Diana?" cried Anne. "Has your mother relented at last?"

"Oh, Anne, do come quick," implored Diana. "Minnie May is awful sick – she's got croup, Mary Jo says. Father and mother are away to town and there's nobody to go for the doctor and Mary Jo doesn't know what to do and – oh, Anne, I'm so scared."

Matthew, without a word, reached out for cap and coat, slipped past Diana and away into the darkness of the yard.

"He's gone to harness the sorrel mare to go to Carmody for the doctor," said Anne, who was hurrying into hood and jacket. "I know it as well as if he'd said so. Matthew and I are such kindred spirits I can read his thoughts without words at all."

"What if he doesn't find the doctor in Carmody?" Diana sobbed. "Mary Jo never saw anybody with croup and she doesn't know what to do. Oh, Anne!"

"Don't cry, Di," said Anne cheerily. "I know exactly what to do for croup. Mrs. Hammond's twins had it three times. Just wait 'til I get the ipecac bottle – in case you don't have any in your house. Come on now."

The two girls hastened out hand in hand, hurried up the lane and across the crusted field, for the snow was too deep to go by the shorter way through the woods.

Minnie May, aged three, was really very sick. She lay on the kitchen sofa, feverish and restless. Her hoarse breathing could be heard all over the house. Mary Jo, a big, broad-faced girl, whom Mrs. Barry had engaged to stay with the children, was helpless and bewildered, quite incapable of deciding what to do.

Anne went to work with skill and promptness. "Minnie May has croup all right. She's pretty bad but I've seen worse. First we must have lots of hot water. Mary Jo, you put some wood in the stove. I'll undress Minnie May and put her to bed. Diana, you try to find some soft flannel cloths. I'm going to give her a dose of ipecac first of all."

Minnie May did not take kindly to the ipecac but Anne had not brought up three pairs of twins for nothing. Down went the ipecac, not only once but many times during the long, anxious night. It was three o'clock when Matthew came with the doctor, for he had been obliged to go all the way to Spencervale. But the need for assistance was past. Minnie May was

much better and sleeping soundly.

"I was awfully near to giving up in despair," explained Anne. "She got worse and worse until she was sicker than ever the Hammond twins were. I actually thought she was going to choke to death. I gave her every drop of ipecac in that bottle and when the last dose went down I said to myself – not to Diana or Mary Jo because I didn't want to worry them – but I said to myself 'this is the last lingering hope.' But in about three minutes she coughed up the phlegm and began to get better right away. You must just imagine my relief, doctor, because I can't express it in words."

The doctor looked at Anne as though he were thinking things about *her* that couldn't be expressed in words, either.

Anne went home in the wonderful, white-frosted winter morning, heavy-eyed from loss of sleep, but still talking to Matthew as they crossed the long, white field and crossed under the glittering fairy arch of the maples in the lane.

"Oh, Matthew, isn't it a wonderful morning? I'm so glad we live in a world that has white frosts. And I'm so glad Mrs. Hammond had three pairs of twins.

If she hadn't, I might never have known what to do for Minnie May. But, oh, I'm so sleepy. I can't go to school. I just know I couldn't keep my eyes open. But I hate to stay home in case Gil – some of the others get ahead of the class. It's so hard to catch up again."

"Well now, I guess you'll manage all right," said Matthew, looking at Anne's white face and the dark shadows under her eyes. "You just go right to bed and have a good sleep. I'll do all the chores."

Anne slept so long and so soundly that it was well on in the white and rosy winter afternoon when she awoke and descended to the kitchen where Marilla, who had arrived home in the meantime, was sitting knitting.

"Matthew has been telling me about last night. I must say it was fortunate you knew what to do. I wouldn't have had any idea, myself. I never saw a case of croup. There now, have your dinner before you tell me about it."

When Anne had finished everything, right down to the dish of blue plums, Marilla said, "Mrs. Barry was here this afternoon. She wanted to see you but I wouldn't wake you up. The doctor told her you saved Minnie May's life – that it would have been too late by

the time he got there. She says she's very sorry she acted the way she did about the currant wine and she hopes you'll forgive her and be good friends with Diana again."

Anne jumped up, her face glowing. "Oh, Marilla, can I go up to the Barrys' right now – without washing my dishes? I'll wash them when I come back but I cannot tie myself down to something so unromantic as dishwashing at this thrilling moment."

"Yes, yes, run along," said Marilla indulgently. "Anne Shirley – are you crazy? Put something warm on. You'll catch your death of cold!"

Anne came dancing home in the purple winter twilight. "You see before you a perfectly happy person, Marilla," she announced. "I'm perfectly happy – yes, in spite of my red hair. Mrs. Barry kissed me and cried and said she was so sorry and she could never repay me. I felt fearfully embarrassed but I just said as politely as I could, 'I have no hard feelings for you, Mrs. Barry. I assure you once for all that I did not mean to intoxicate Diana and henceforth I shall cover the past with the mantle of oblivion.' That was a pretty dignified way of speaking, wasn't it, Marilla? And Diana and I had a lovely afternoon. Then Mrs. Barry served tea on the very best china set just as if I was real company. And when I came home Diana stood at the window and threw kisses at me all the way down the lane. And tonight, Marilla, I'm going to make up a special brand-new prayer in honour of the occasion."

6

Anne went on feeling she was a perfectly happy person all through the winter and spring. Little mistakes such as absentmindedly emptying a pan of skim milk into the basket of yarn balls in the pantry, when it was supposed to go into the pigs' bucket, and walking clean over the edge of the log bridge into the brook while wrapped in a daydream, were not really worth counting. Not even accidentally mixing liniment into the cake she was making for the minister's visit counted as getting into real trouble. Then Diana gave a party.

"Small and select," Anne assured Marilla. "Just the girls in our class."

They had a very good time and nothing untoward happened until after tea, when they found themselves in the Barry garden, a little tired of all their games and ripe for some enticing form of mischief.

Marilla was in the orchard picking a panful of summer apples when Mr. Barry came up the slope carrying a limp Anne whose head lolled against his shoulder. A whole procession of little girls trailed after them.

"What's happened to her?" Marilla gasped, shaken and white.

Anne herself answered, lifting her head. "Don't be frightened, Marilla. Josie Pye dared me to walk the ridgepole of Barrys' kitchen roof and I fell off. I expect I've sprained my ankle. But, Marilla, I might have broken my neck. Let us look on the bright side."

Marilla let out a sharp sigh of relief. "I might have known you'd go and do something of that sort. Bring her in here, Mr. Barry, and lay her on the sofa. Mercy, the child's fainted."

Matthew, hastily summoned from the harvest field, was straightway sent for the doctor, who announced, when he finally arrived, that the injury was more serious than they had supposed. Anne's ankle was broken.

That night, when Marilla went up to the east

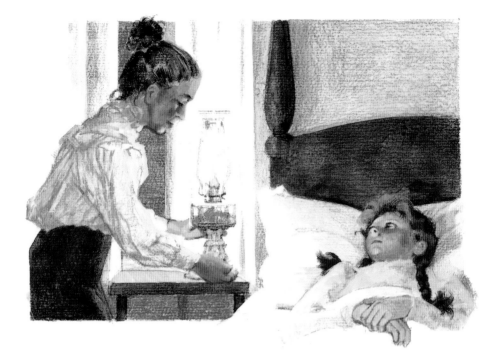

gable where a white-faced girl was lying, a plaintive voice greeted her from the bed. "Aren't you sorry for me, Marilla?"

"It was your own fault," said Marilla, twitching down the blind and lighting a lamp.

"And that's just why you should be sorry for me," said Anne, "because the thought that it *is* my fault is what makes it so hard. If I could blame it on anybody I would feel so much better. But what would you have done if you'd been dared to walk a ridge-pole?"

"I'd have stayed on good firm ground and let

them dare away. Such absurdity!"

Anne sighed. "But you have such strength of mind, Marilla. I haven't. I just felt I couldn't bear Josie Pye's scorn. She would have crowed over me all my life. And I've been punished so much you needn't be cross with me, Marilla. It's not a bit nice to faint. And the doctor hurt me dreadfully when he set my ankle. Oh, I am an afflicted mortal. But I'll try to bear it bravely if only you won't be cross with me, Marilla."

"There, there, I'm not cross. You're an unlucky child, there's no doubt of that. But as you say, you'll have the suffering of it. Here now, try and eat some supper."

"Isn't it fortunate I've got such an imagination? It will help me through splendidly."

Anne had good reason to bless her imagination during the tedious seven weeks that followed. But she was not solely dependent on it. She had many visitors and not a day passed without one or more of the girls dropping in to bring her flowers and books and tell her all the happenings in the juvenile world of Avonlea.

"What do you think, Marilla?" Anne said one day when Diana had been to visit. "The school trustees have hired a new teacher and it's a lady. Miss Muriel Stacy. Isn't that a romantic name? And oh, Marilla, I'll miss her first weeks at school. She won't be new anymore by the time I get to go to school and Gil – everybody will be ahead of me in class. Oh, I shall be so glad when I can go to school. Diana says she has the loveliest fair curly hair and such fascinating eyes. She dresses beautifully and her sleeve puffs are bigger than anybody else's in Avonlea."

"There's one thing plain to be seen, Anne," said Marilla. "Your fall off the Barry roof hasn't injured your tongue at all."

It was October before Anne was ready to go back to school – a glorious October, all red and gold with mellow mornings when the valleys were filled with delicate mists. The dews were so heavy that the fields glistened like cloth of silver. There was a tang in the air that inspired the hearts of small maidens tripping swiftly and willingly to school. It *was* jolly to be back again in the little brown desk beside Diana with Ruby Gillis nodding across the aisle and Carrie Sloane sending up notes and Julia Bell sending a 'chew' of gum down from the back seat. Anne drew a long breath of happiness as she sharpened her pencil and arranged her picture cards on her desk. Life was certainly very interesting.

Miss Stacy proved another true and helpful friend and under her influence Anne expanded like a flower as she carried home for the admiring Matthew and the critical Marilla glowing accounts of school work.

"I love Miss Stacy with my whole heart, Marilla. She is so ladylike and she has such a sweet voice. When she pronounces my name I feel *instinctively* that she's spelling it with an 'e'. We had recitations this afternoon. I wish you could have been there to hear me recite "Mary, Queen of Scots." I just put my whole soul into it. Ruby Gillis told me it just made her blood run cold."

"Well now, you might just recite it for me some of these days, out in the barn," suggested Matthew.

"Of course I will, but I won't be able to do it so well," said Anne meditatively. "It won't be so exciting as it is when you have a whole schoolful before you hanging breathlessly on your words. I know I won't be able to make your blood run cold."

"Mrs. Lynde says it made *her* blood run cold to see the boys climbing after crows' nests last Friday,"

said Marilla. "I wonder at Miss Stacy for encouraging it."

"But we needed a crow's nest for nature study," explained Anne. "That was on our field afternoon. Field afternoons are splendid, Marilla. And Miss Stacy explains everything so beautifully. We have to write compositions on our field afternoons and I write the best ones."

"It's very vain of you to say so then. You'd better let your teacher say it."

"But she *did* say it, Marilla. And indeed I'm *not* vain about it. How can I be when I'm such a dunce at geometry? Although I'm really beginning to see through it a little, too. Miss Stacy makes it so clear. Still, I'll never be good at it and I assure you it is a very humbling reflection. But I love writing compositions. We have physical culture exercises every day, too. They make you graceful and promote digestion."

"Promote fiddlesticks!" said Marilla. "Just so much nonsense."

But all the field afternoons and recitation Fridays and physical culture contortions paled before Miss Stacy's November proposal – that the scholars of Avonlea school should get up a concert and hold it in the hall on Christmas night to help pay for the school flag. The preparations for the program were begun at once and Anne threw herself into them heart and soul, hampered though she was by Marilla's disapproval. Marilla thought it all rank foolishness.

"It's just filling your heads up with nonsense and taking time that ought to be put on your lessons," she grumbled. "I don't approve of children getting up concerts and racing about to practices. It makes them vain and forward and fond of gadding."

"But think of the worthy object," pleaded Anne. "A flag will cultivate a spirit of patriotism."

"Fudge! There's precious little patriotism in the thoughts of any of you. All you want is a good time."

"Well, when you can combine patriotism and fun isn't it all right? We're going to have six choruses and Diana is to sing a solo. I'm in two dialogues and I'm to have two recitations, Marilla. I just tremble when I think of it, but it's a nice thrilly kind of tremble. And we're to have a tableau at the end, 'Faith,

Hope and Charity.' Diana, Ruby and I are to be in it, all draped in white with flowing hair. Oh, Marilla, I know you are not enthusiastic about it, but as I *am*, don't you hope your Anne will distinguish herself?"

"All I hope is that you'll behave yourself. I'll be heartily glad when all this fuss is over and you'll be able to settle down. You are simply good for nothing with your head stuffed full of dialogues and tableaus. As for your tongue, it's a marvel it's not clean worn out."

Anne sighed and went off to the backyard over which a new moon shone through the leafless poplar boughs, and where Matthew was splitting wood. Anne perched herself on a block and talked it over with him.

"Well now, I reckon it's going to be a pretty good concert. And I expect you'll do your part fine," he said, smiling down into her eager, vivacious little face.

Anne smiled back at him. Matthew was truly a kindred spirit. She'd known it from the first moment she'd seen him.

7

Christmas morning broke on a beautiful white world. It had been a very mild December and people had looked forward to a green Christmas; but just enough snow fell softly in the night to transfigure Avonlea. Anne peeped from her frosted gable window with delighted eyes. The firs in the woods were all feathery and wonderful; the birches and wild cherry trees were outlined in pearl; the ploughed fields were stretches of snowy dimples; and the crisp tang in the air was glorious.

Anne ran downstairs singing until her voice re-echoed through Green Gables.

"Merry Christmas, Marilla! Merry Christmas, Matthew! Isn't it a lovely Christmas? I'm so glad it's white. Any other kind of Christmas doesn't seem real, does it?" She stopped suddenly as Matthew, with a sheepish look at Marilla, brought something out from behind his back and held it up.

"Why Matthew, a dress! Is that for me? Oh, Matthew!" Anne took the dress and gazed at it in reverent silence. How pretty it was – a lovely soft brown gloria with all the gloss of silk; a skirt with dainty frills and shirrings; a waist elaborately pin-tucked in the most fashionable way, with a little ruffle of filmy lace at the neck. But the sleeves! Long elbow cuffs and above them two beautiful puffs divided by rows of shirring and ribbon bows.

"Why – why – Anne," Matthew said shyly, "don't you like it? Well now – well now."

For Anne's eyes had suddenly filled with tears. "Like it! Oh, Matthew!" Anne laid the dress over a chair and clasped her hands. "Matthew, it's perfectly exquisite. I can never thank you enough. Oh, it seems to me this must be a happy dream."

"Well, well, let us have breakfast," interrupted Marilla. "I must say, Anne, I don't think you need the dress but since Matthew has got it for you, see you take good care of it. There's a lot of material wasted in those sleeves."

"I don't see how I'm going to eat breakfast," said Anne rapturously. "Breakfast seems so commonplace at such an exciting moment. I'd rather feast my eyes on that dress. I'm so glad puffed sleeves are still fashionable. I'd never get over it if they went out before I had a dress with them. I feel that I ought to be a very good girl indeed. It's at times like this I'm sorry I'm not a model girl but I really will make an extra effort after this."

All the Avonlea scholars were in a fever of excitement that day, for the hall had to be decorated and a last grand rehearsal held.

The concert came off in the evening and was pronounced a success. The little hall was crowded; all the performers did excellently well but Anne was the bright particular star of the occasion, as even envy, in the shape of Josie Pye, dared not deny.

"Oh, hasn't it been a brilliant evening?" sighed Anne when it was all over and she and Diana were walking home together under a dark, starry sky.

"Everything went off very well," said Diana practically. "I guess we must have made as much as ten dollars and the minister is going to send an account of it to the Charlottetown papers."

"Oh, Diana, will we really see our names in print? It makes me thrill to think of it. Your solo was perfectly elegant. I felt prouder than you did when it was encored. I just said to myself, 'It is my dear bosom friend who is so honoured.' "

"Well, your recitations just brought down the house, Anne. That sad one was simply splendid."

"I was so nervous, Diana. When Miss Stacy called out my name I really cannot tell how I ever got up on that platform. For one dreadful moment I was sure I couldn't begin at all. Then I thought of my lovely puffed sleeves and took courage."

"Wasn't the boys' dialogue fine?" said Diana. "Gilbert Blythe was just splendid. And wait till I tell you, Anne. When you ran off the platform after the fairy dialogue one of your roses fell out of your hair. I saw Gil pick it up and put it in his breast pocket. There now. You're so romantic that I'm sure you ought to be pleased by that."

"It is really nothing to me what that person does,

Diana," said Anne loftily.

"I do think it's awful mean the way you treat Gil."

"I simply never waste a single thought on him. Tell me – in the second narration, did I groan all right?"

Avonlea school found it hard to settle down to a humdrum existence again. To Anne in particular, things seemed fearfully flat, stale and unprofitable.

"I'm positively certain, Diana, that life can never be quite the same again. I'm afraid concerts spoil people for everyday life. I suppose that's why Marilla disapproves of them."

Eventually, however, Avonlea school took up old interests. That spring Miss Stacy decided they would study Tennyson's poem about King Arthur. For months they analysed and parsed and generally tore it to pieces until Lancelot and Guinevere and King Arthur and Elaine the fair lily maid had become real people to them. Anne was consumed by the secret regret that she had not been born in Camelot, so one day she suggested they dramatize the story of the lily maid floating down the river.

"Of course *you* must be Elaine, Anne," said Diana.

"But it's so ridiculous to have a redheaded Elaine," Anne mourned. "Ruby ought to be Elaine because she has such lovely long golden hair."

"Oh, no," said Ruby with a shiver. "I wouldn't mind floating down in the boat if I could sit up. But to lie down and pretend I was dead – I just couldn't."

"Well . . . I'll be Elaine," said Anne reluctantly. "Ruby, you must be King Arthur and Jane will be Guinevere and Diana, Lancelot. We'll use your father's old dory, Diana. And we must have a pall. That old, black shawl of your mother's, Diana." Diana ran for the shawl and Anne spread it over the flat-bottomed boat and then lay down on it, with closed eyes and hands folded over her breast.

"Oh, she really does look dead," whispered Ruby Gillis nervously. "It makes me feel frightened."

"Stop being silly, Ruby," said Anne. "Jane, you'll have to arrange everything. It's silly for me to be talking when I'm Elaine and she's dead."

Jane rose to the occasion, draping a yellow piano scarf over Anne for the cloth of gold and, since no white lilies were in bloom, placing a tall blue iris in one of Anne's folded hands.

"Now she's all ready," Jane announced. "We must

kiss her quiet brows and say 'Sister, farewell for ever.' That's right. Now, push her off!"

The boat scraped roughly over stones and an embedded stake, then was caught by the current and headed toward the bridge. The girls scampered through the woods, across the road and down to the headland where, as King Arthur, Lancelot and Guinevere, they would be ready to receive the lily maid.

At first Anne, drifting slowly down the stream, enjoyed the romance of her situation to the full. Then she started to feel a creeping chill. Scrambling to her feet, and picking up her cloth-of-gold coverlet and black pall, she gazed blankly at a big crack in the bottom of her barge through which water was pouring. She must get to shore. Where were the oars? Left behind at the landing!

Anne gave one gasping little scream which nobody heard; she was white to the lips but she did not lose her self-possession. There was one chance – just one. "Dear God," she prayed over and over, "let me float close enough to one of the bridge piles."

The water climbed higher and higher. Then, just as the dory seemed ready to sink, it bumped against a bridge pile. Anne scrambled up on the slippery wood and, clinging as tightly as she could, watched her barge drift under the bridge and sink in midstream.

Minutes passed, each seeming an hour to the lily maid. Why didn't somebody come? Where had the girls gone? Suppose she grew so cramped and tired that she could hold on no longer? Anne stared into the wicked green depths below, her imagination suggesting all manner of gruesome possibilities.

Then, just as she thought she really could not endure the ache in her arms and wrists another moment, Gilbert Blythe came rowing under the bridge!

"Anne Shirley, how on earth did you get there?" Without waiting for an answer he pulled close to her perch and extended his hand. Anne scrambled down into the dory, where she sat dripping and furious, with her arms full of wet shawl and scarf.

"What happened, Anne?" asked Gilbert, taking up his oars.

"We were playing Elaine," Anne explained frigidly, without even looking at her rescuer, "and I had to drift down to Camelot in the barge – dory – and it began to leak. Will you be kind enough to row me to the landing?"

Gilbert obliged, and Anne, disdaining assistance, sprang nimbly onto the shore.

"I'm very much obliged to you," she said haughtily as she turned away. But Gilbert had also sprung from the boat and now laid a hand on her arm.

"Look here, Anne," he said hurriedly, "can't we be friends? I'm awfully sorry I made fun of your hair that time. It was only a joke. Besides, it's so long ago. I think your hair is awfully pretty now – honest I do. Let's be friends."

For a moment Anne hesitated. She looked at the half-shy, half-eager expression in Gilbert's hazel eyes and her heart gave a quick, queer little beat. Then that scene of two years before flashed back into her mind. "No," she said coldly, "I shall never be friends with you, Gilbert Blythe."

"All right, then!" Gilbert sprang into his skiff with an angry colour in his cheeks. "I'll never ask you to be friends again, Anne Shirley."

He pulled away with swift, defiant strokes, and Anne went up the steep, ferny path under the maples. She held her head high, but she was conscious of an odd feeling of regret. She almost wished she had answered Gilbert differently. Of course, he had insulted her terribly, but still . . . ! Altogether, Anne thought it would be a relief to sit down and have a good cry.

8

It was nearly dark. The dull November twilight had fallen around Green Gables and the only light in the kitchen came from the dancing red flames in the stove.

Anne was curled up on the hearth-rug gazing into that joyous glow. She had been reading, but her book slipped to the floor, and now she was dreaming. Glittering castles in Spain were shaping themselves out of the mists and rainbows of her lively fancy.

Marilla watched Anne tenderly for a time, then laid her knitting on her lap. "Miss Stacy was here this afternoon when you were out with Diana," she said.

Anne came back from her other world with a start and a sigh. "Was she? Oh, I'm so sorry I wasn't in. Why didn't you call me? Diana and I were only over in the woods. Why did she come?"

"She wants to organize a class among her advanced students – an extra hour after school to study for the entrance examination into Queen's Academy. And she came to ask Matthew and me if we would like to have you join it. What do you think, Anne? Would you like to go to Queen's and pass for a teacher?"

"Oh, Marilla!" Anne clasped her hands. "It's been the dream of my life – that is, for the last six months since Jane and Ruby began to talk about studying for the entrance. But I didn't say anything about it, because I supposed it would be perfectly useless. I'd love to be a teacher. But won't it be dreadfully expensive?"

"I guess you needn't worry about that part of it. When Matthew and I took you to bring you up we resolved we would do the best we could for you. I

believe in a girl being fitted to earn her own living whether she has to or not. As long as Matthew and I are here, you'll always have a home at Green Gables, but nobody knows what's going to happen in this uncertain world and it's just as well to be prepared. So you can join the Queen's class if you like, Anne."

"Oh, Marilla, thank you." Anne flung her arms around Marilla's waist and looked up earnestly into her face. "I'm extremely grateful to you and Matthew, and I'll study as hard as I can and do my very best to be a credit to you. But I warn you not to expect too much in geometry."

"I dare say you'll get along well enough. Miss Stacy says you're bright and diligent." Marilla hesitated for a moment, then said, "You're real steady and reliable now, Anne. I used to think you'd never get over your featherbrained ways but now – well, I wouldn't be afraid to trust you in anything." She had to clear her throat before she could add in her usual brisk tones, "And anyway, there's no rush. You won't be ready to write the exams for a year and a half yet."

"I shall take more interest than ever in my studies now," said Anne blissfully, "because I have a purpose in life. Just last Sunday in church the minister said everyone should have a worthy purpose in life and pursue it faithfully. I would call it a worthy purpose to want to be a teacher like Miss Stacy, wouldn't you, Marilla?"

The Queen's class was organized in due time – seven students in all. Anne had expected that Gilbert Blythe and Josie Pye would be included but it seemed like nothing short of a calamity when she heard that Diana's parents didn't intend to send her to Queen's and couldn't see the use of all that studying. On the evening when the Queen's class first stayed behind for extra lessons and Anne saw Diana go slowly out with the others, it was all she could do to keep her seat.

"Oh, Marilla," she said later. "I really felt that I had tasted the bitterness of death when I saw her start off to walk home alone. How splendid it would have been if Diana had only been studying Entrance, too. But I guess the minister's right. We can't have things perfect in this imperfect world. And I do think the Queen's class is going to be extremely interesting. Jane and Ruby are going to study to be teachers. Charlie says he's going into politics. Josie Pye says she is going to college for education's sake because she won't have to earn her own living; she says, of course,

it is different with orphans who are living on charity –
they have to hustle." Anne tossed her braids to show
her opinion of Josie Pye.

"What is Gilbert Blythe going to be?" asked
Marilla, as Anne started to open her Latin grammar.

"I don't happen to know what Gilbert Blythe's
ambition in life is – if he has any," said Anne scorn-
fully.

Anne and Gilbert were open rivals now. Previ-
ously the rivalry had been rather one-sided, but now
there was no longer any doubt that Gilbert was as
determined to be first in class as Anne was.

Outside the classroom, Gilbert talked and jested
with the other girls, exchanged books and puzzles
with them, discussed lessons and plans, sometimes
walked them home. But Anne Shirley might not have
existed for all the attention he paid her.

All at once, to Anne's secret dismay, she found

the old resentment against him gone. In vain she recalled every moment of that early humiliation, tried to feel the old satisfying anger. It had gone without a flicker – she had forgiven and forgotten without realizing it. Her one consolation was that neither Gilbert nor anybody else, not even Diana, should ever suspect how sorry she was or how much she wished she hadn't been so proud and horrid!

Otherwise the winter slipped away pleasantly. There were lessons to be learned, honours to be won, delightful books to be read, new pieces to be practised for the Sunday School choir and before Anne knew it, the first year of the Queen's class was over.

Anne started the summer tired and heavy-eyed. The Spencervale doctor who had come the night Minnie May had the croup warned Marilla, "Keep that redheaded girl of yours out in the open air all summer and don't let her read books until she gets more spring in her step." Marilla, fearful that Anne might die of consumption, shooed Anne outside where she walked, rowed, berried and dreamed to her heart's content. It would have been a perfect summer if the doctor hadn't had to come again.

"Matthew's had another bad spell with his heart,"

Marilla explained, when Anne came running to find out why the doctor's horse and buggy were just pulling out of Green Gables lane. "The doctor says he's not to do any more heavy work. You might as well tell Matthew not to breathe as not to work." Marilla tightened her lips at the thought of her brother's quiet stubbornness. But the bad spell passed and Matthew seemed to be his old self again.

In the autumn, Miss Stacy found all her pupils eager for work once more. The Queen's class especially squared their shoulders for the fray, for at the end of the year loomed that fateful thing known as "the Entrance Exam." Suppose they did not pass? That thought haunted Anne through the entire winter and gave her bad dreams in which she stared miserably at pass lists of the Entrance exams where Gilbert Blythe's name was blazoned at the top and hers did not appear at all.

But it was a jolly, busy, happy, swift-flying winter. New worlds of thought and ambition seemed to be opening before Anne's eager eyes. Miss Stacy led her class to think, explore and discover for themselves. And Anne expanded socially, too, for Marilla, mindful of the Spencervale doctor's advice, no longer vetoed the occasional outings. So there were sleigh drives and skating frolics galore.

Anne was shooting up so rapidly that Marilla was startled one day, as they stood side by side, to find herself looking up at the girl. There was another change – Anne had become much quieter. Marilla noticed this and commented.

"You don't chatter as much as you used to, Anne, nor use half so many big words. What has come over you?"

Anne coloured and laughed a little, as she dropped her book and gazed dreamily out the window, where big fat red buds were bursting out on the vine. "I don't know – I don't *want* to talk as much. It's nicer to keep thoughts in one's heart like treasures. I don't like having them laughed at or wondered over. And somehow I don't want to use big words any more – Miss Stacy says the short ones are much stronger. She makes us write all our essays as simply as possible. It was hard at first, but I've got used to it and now I see it's so much better."

"You've only two more months before the Entrance exams. Do you think you'll be able to get through?"

Anne shivered. "I don't know. Sometimes I think I'll be all right – and then I get horribly afraid. We've studied hard and Miss Stacy has drilled us thoroughly, but we've each got a stumbling block. Mine is geometry. Miss Stacy is going to give us exams in June just as hard as the Entrance, so we'll have some idea of what they'll be like. But it haunts me, Marilla. What will I do if I fail?"

"Why go to school next year and try again," said Marilla unconcernedly.

"Oh, I don't believe I'd have the heart for that." Anne sighed and, dragging her eyes from the green things upspringing in the garden, buried herself resolutely in her books.

9

The Monday after Avonlea School closed for the summer all the Queen's class travelled to town for their week of exams. By Tuesday, Anne felt so homesick she had to write it all down.

Dearest Diana,

Last night I was horribly lonesome all alone in my room and wished so much you were with me. This morning Miss Stacy came for me and we walked to the Academy, calling for Jane and Ruby and Josie on our way. Josie said I looked as though I hadn't slept a wink. There are times when I don't feel I've made much headway in learning to like Josie Pye.

At the Academy, there were scores of students from all over the Island. When we were assigned our rooms, Miss Stacy had to leave us. Jane and I sat together and Jane was so composed that I envied her. Then a man came in and started distributing the English examination sheets. My hands grew cold and my head fairly whirled as I picked mine up. Just one awful moment – and then everything cleared up, and I knew I could do something with *that* paper anyway.

Oh, Diana, if only the geometry examination were over!

Yours devotedly,
Anne

A tired Anne arrived home on Friday evening in chastened triumph, to find Diana at Green Gables to welcome her back.

"It seems an age since you went to town, Anne. How did you do?"

"Pretty well, I think, in everything but geometry. Oh, how good it is to be back. Green Gables is the dearest, loveliest spot in the world."

"How did the others do?"

"Josie says the geometry was so easy a child of ten could do it! Ruby says she knows she didn't pass, but I think she did pretty well. Charlie thinks he failed history." The name of Gilbert Blythe hung in the air between them but Anne refused to say it. She and

Gilbert had met and passed each other on the street a dozen times that week without any sign of recognition. Each time Anne had held her head a little higher and wished a little more earnestly that she had made friends with Gilbert when he asked her.

After two weeks Anne took to haunting the post office. After three weeks with no pass list appearing, she began to feel she couldn't stand the strain much longer. But one evening as she sat at her window drinking in the beauty of the summer dusk, she saw Diana flying up the slope with a newspaper fluttering in her hand.

"Anne, you've passed, " she cried, "passed the very first – you and Gilbert both – you're ties – but *your* name is first. Oh, I'm so proud!"

Anne snatched up the paper. Yes, she *had* passed. There was her name at the top of a list of two hundred.

"I'm just dazzled inside," said Anne. "I want to say a hundred things but I can't find the words. I must run out to the field and tell Matthew."

They hurried to the hayfield where, as luck would have it, they found Marilla, too.

"I've passed!" Anne exclaimed, waving the paper. "First – or, at least one of the first."

"Well now, I always said it," said Matthew, gazing at the pass list delightedly. "I knew you could beat them all easy."

"You've done pretty well, I must say, Anne." But the proud look on Marilla's face told Anne more than the cool words.

That night Anne knelt by her open window in a great sheen of moonlight and murmured a prayer that came right from her heart – a prayer of thankfulness for the past and hope for the future.

In no time at all the summer was over and Anne

was packing to go to Queen's Academy. On her last evening, as she was sorting books into her trunk, Marilla came into the east gable, her arms full of a delicate pale green material.

"Anne, here's a nice light dress for you. I thought you'd like something real dressy to wear if you were asked out of an evening in town. I hear Jane and Ruby and Josie have got evening dresses and I don't mean you should be behind them."

"Oh, Marilla, it's lovely," Anne said as she shook out the shirrings and frills. "You shouldn't be so kind to me. It makes it harder to go away."

She put the dress on and went down to the kitchen to show Matthew. "Perfect for a recitation," she laughed and started into "The Maiden's Vow," a piece she had learned for the school concert. As she finished she looked up to see tears in Marilla's eyes.

"I declare, my recitation has made you cry," she said gaily, stooping over Marilla's chair to drop a butterfly kiss on that lady's cheek.

"Not your poetry," Marilla protested. "I just couldn't help thinking of the little girl you used to be with all your queer ways. You look so different in that dress. As though you didn't belong in Avonlea – I just got lonesome thinking it all over."

"Marilla!" Anne sat down on Marilla's gingham lap and took the lined face between her hands. "I'm not a bit changed. I'm only just pruned down and branched out. At heart, I'll always be your little Anne who will love you and Matthew and Green Gables more and better every day of her life."

"Well now," said Matthew hoarsely, "I guess she ain't been much spoiled, Marilla. I guess my putting in my oar occasional never did much harm after all."

"You do like to rub things in, Matthew Cuthbert!" Marilla retorted.

Anne returned in triumph from her year at the Academy. She had won the scholarship that would pay her way to Redmond College. Several of the boys would be going on to college as well, while Ruby and Josie were going to teach in schools nearby.

"Gilbert Blythe is going to teach, too," Diana told Anne, as they sat in the east gable room on Anne's first night home. "He has to. His father can't afford to send him to college next year after all, so he means to earn his own way."

Anne felt a queer sensation of dismayed surprise. She had expected Gilbert would be going to Redmond, too. What would she do without her friend the enemy?

The next morning at breakfast it suddenly struck Anne that Matthew was looking much greyer than the year before.

"Marilla," she said hesitatingly when he had gone out, "is Matthew quite well?"

"No, he isn't." Marilla's voice was troubled. "He's had some real bad spells with his heart this spring and he won't spare himself a mite. We've got a real good hired man now, so I'm hoping he'll kind of rest and pick up."

"You're not looking well yourself, Marilla. You must rest while I do the work."

Marilla smiled affectionately at her girl. "It's not the work – it's my head. I've a pain so often now behind my eyes I can't read or sew with any comfort. These glasses don't do me any good. The doctor says I must see an oculist when he comes to the Island at the end of June."

That evening, Anne wandered out to meet Matthew as he walked slowly up the lane behind the cows, his head bent.

"You've been working too hard, Matthew," she said reproachfully. "Why won't you take things easier?"

"Well now, I can't seem to," Matthew replied as he opened the yard gate to let the cows through. "It's only that I'm getting old, Anne."

"If I'd been the boy you'd sent for," said Anne wistfully, "I'd be able to help you so much now and spare you in a hundred ways."

"Well now, I'd rather have you than a dozen boys, Anne," said Matthew, patting her hand. "Just mind you that – rather than a dozen boys." He smiled his shy smile at her and went into the yard.

Anne took the memory of that smile with her when she went to her room that night, and sat at her open window thinking of the past and dreaming of the future.

10

"Matthew – Matthew – what's the matter? Matthew, are you sick?" It was Marilla who spoke, alarm in every jerky word. Anne, coming through the hall, her hands full of white narcissus, saw Matthew standing in the porch doorway, his face strangely drawn and grey. She dropped her flowers and sprang across the kitchen to him at the same moment as Marilla. Before they could reach him, Matthew had fallen across the threshold.

"He's fainted," gasped Marilla. "Run for Martin, he's in the barn."

Martin, the hired man, started at once for the doctor, calling at the Barrys' on his way. The Barrys found Anne and Marilla trying to revive Matthew. Mr. Barry felt for a pulse, then looked at their anxious faces sorrowfully.

"I don't think there's anything we can do for him."

"Mr. Barry, you don't think . . ." Anne could not say the dreadful word.

"Child, I'm afraid so."

The news spread quickly through Avonlea and all day friends and neighbours came and went on errands of kindness for the dead and the living. For the first time, shy, quiet Matthew Cuthbert was a person of central importance.

As the calm night came softly over Green Gables Matthew lay in his coffin in the parlour, surrounded by flowers Anne had gathered to lay about him. Although Diana came up to the east gable with her, Anne wanted to be alone. It was early morning before tears came and Anne wept her heart out. Marilla, hearing, crept in to comfort her.

"There, there, dearie. Don't cry so. Tears won't bring him back."

"Oh, Marilla, what will we do without him?"

"We've got each other. I don't know what I'd do if you weren't here – if you'd never come. I know I've been kind of strict and harsh with you maybe – but you mustn't think that I didn't love you as much as

Matthew did. It's never been easy to say things out of my heart but I want to tell you now, you've been my joy and comfort ever since you came to Green Gables."

Two days later they carried Matthew Cuthbert over his homestead threshold, away from the fields he had tilled, the orchards he had loved and the trees he had planted. Then Avonlea settled back to its usual placidity and, even at Green Gables, affairs slipped into their old groove.

One afternoon in late summer, Marilla came slowly in from the yard where she had been talking with a caller.

"What did Mr. Sadler want, Marilla?"

Marilla sat down by the window with tears in her eyes. "He heard I was going to sell Green Gables and he wants to buy it."

"Sell Green Gables? Oh, Marilla, you don't mean it!"

"Anne, I don't know what else to do. If my eyes were strong . . . But you know what the oculist said – my sight may go altogether. How would I run things alone?" Marilla broke down and wept bitterly.

"You won't have to be here alone. I'll be

with you."

Marilla lifted her worn face from her hands. "What do you mean?"

"I'm not going to Redmond College. I decided so the night you came home from seeing the oculist. You surely don't think I could leave you alone in your trouble, Marilla? I applied to teach at the school over at Carmody, but I just heard this afternoon . . ." Anne paused, then said in a rush, "Gilbert Blythe turned down the Avonlea school and asked the trustees to hire me instead. So you see, you shan't be dull or lonesome. We'll be real cozy and happy here together."

"Oh, Anne. I could get on real well if you were here. But I can't let you sacrifice yourself for me."

"Nonsense." Anne laughed merrily. "Nothing could be worse than giving up Green Gables."

"But your ambitions – and – "

"Oh, I've changed my ambitions. I'm going to be a good teacher – and I'm going to save your eyesight. And I'll study here at home."

"I don't feel I ought to let you give up the scholarship you won."

"But you can't prevent me. I'm sixteen and a half

and as obstinate as a mule. Don't pity me, Marilla. There's no need. When I left Queen's my future seemed to stretch out like a straight road. Now there's a bend in it. I don't know what lies around the bend, but I'm going to believe that the best does."

Anne sat long at her window that night. The wind purred softly in the cherry boughs as she thought about how much her life had changed. Just that morning she had met Gilbert on the road. She felt herself blushing as she remembered holding out her hand, offering a hesitant apology for the years she had held that stubborn grudge.

"It's time we were friends, Anne," Gilbert had replied.

Anne looked up at the stars twinkling over the pointed firs in the hollow. "God's in his heaven, all's right with the world," she whispered softly.